About the Book

Roots and berries, roots and berries. Mr. Wolf is sick of eating roots and berries. He sets out early one morning to catch a good supper.

Grandfather Goat says he wouldn't mind being eaten if Mr. Wolf had a fork. As the day goes by, Mr. Wolf catches other animals, but each outsmarts the hungry hunter with a clever story. When night falls, Mr. Wolf has a new fork, soup spoon, and bib—but he still hasn't had a thing for supper.

Here's a funny tale for beginning readers told by Cynthia Jameson in the deft, easy-to-read style she brought to *The Clay Pot Boy* and *Winter Hut*. Mr. Wolf's adventures are gaily illustrated by Ursula Landshoff.

Coward, McCann & Geoghegan, Inc.   *New York*

Mr. Wolf Gets Ready for Supper

by Cynthia Jameson
pictures by Ursula Landshoff

Especially for
NIKOLAI STEPANOVITCH

This morning
Mr. Wolf got out of bed
and rubbed his belly.
How hungry he was!

7

All he had to eat last night
was a small bowl
of roots and berries.

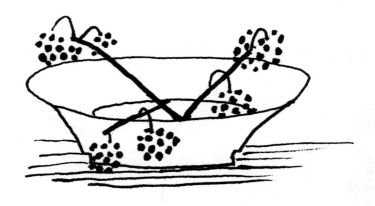

Roots and berries,
roots and berries!
That is all Mr. Wolf
ever brought home for supper.

He was sick of the
very sight of them.
If only he were a good hunter,
he would catch a tasty meal
of rabbit or goose.

But alas,
Mr. Wolf wasn't even clever
enough
to catch a snail.

All the other animals
laughed at him behind his back.
For they knew how to outwit him
with tricks and stories.

"Today is the day,"
said Mr. Wolf to himself.
"I'm going to bring home
a *sc-crumptious* supper."
And as he
walked out the door
he kicked his bowl
of leftover
roots and berries.

It was a lovely morning.
The meadow
was flooded with sunshine
and red and yellow poppies.
But Mr. Wolf
did not have time to notice.
He was slinking along the ground
straining his eyes this way...
and that. . . .

All at once
he spied something moving.
It had a long white beard,
a short white tail,
and two worn-out horns. . . .
It was Grandfather Goat.

Mr. Wolf bounded toward him.
He jumped
on the old goat's back
and growled,
"I've got you now,
Grandfather Goat.

For I'm the clever hunter.
I've got
my teeth
all long and sharp.
And I'm hungry
for goat stew!"

17

Grandfather Goat was terribly shaken.
As soon as he found his voice,
he cried, "Wait!
Don't eat me."

"And why shouldn't I eat you?"
asked Mr. Wolf.

"You haven't got a *fork*,"
said Grandfather Goat.
"I'm old, and I like to see
good manners in others.
Go home this instant
and get a fork.
I'll wait here
till you come back."

"Well-l-l," said Mr. Wolf uncertainly.
"You won't forget
to wait for me, will you?"
"How could I forget?"
replied Grandfather Goat
with a wag of his tail.

As Mr. Wolf hurried home,
he muttered to himself,
"I'll show that old goat
I've got manners."

At once he set about
whittling a fork out of wood.
But it was no simple task.

The only fork
he had ever seen

was the farmer's pitchfork.
And he couldn't
quite
remember
how it looked.

As fast as he could
he ran back to the meadow
where he had
left Grandfather Goat.
But the old fellow
was nowhere in sight.

Mr. Wolf pounded the ground
angrily.
"I knew it!"
he exclaimed.
"That silly old goat
forgot to wait for me."

Having lost one meal,
Mr. Wolf trotted off
with his fork
to look for another.
This time he headed
straight for
the farmer's barnyard.

When he got there,
he saw a sight
that made him drool—
a fine fat goose!
Mr. Wolf
caught her
by the tail feathers.

"I've got you now, Mrs. Goose.
For I'm the clever hunter.
I've got my teeth
all long and sharp.
My fork I whittled out of wood.
And I'm hungry for
a fine fat goose!"
Mrs. Goose squawked with fright.
"Let me go, Mr. Wolf.
You can't eat me."
Mr. Wolf let go.
"Why can't I eat you?
I like goose."
"You'll drop crumbs
on your fur coat,"
said Mrs. Goose.

Mr. Wolf looked down at himself.
Mrs. Goose was right.
He mustn't get crumbs
on his beautiful fur coat.
"What shall I do?"

"Go home and fetch your bib.
Then come back and eat me up,"
clucked Mrs. Goose.

"Well-l-l," considered Mr. Wolf.
"Will the farmer let you stay out
and wait for me?"
"Of course he will, my dear."

So Mr. Wolf hurried home
and set about making a bib.
He tied together cockleburs
and glued them nicely
with mud.

In no time
it was ready.

Carrying his fork
and wearing his bib,
he rushed back
to look for Mrs. Goose.

33

But the barnyard was empty!
There wasn't so much
as an egg in sight.
"Oh, woe," whined Mr. Wolf.

"The farmer must have
taken Mrs. Goose
into the barn.
Now I've lost her forever."

But the day was still young.

And so

Mr. Wolf made off for the forest.

He followed his nose and whiskers

until he arrived at a pond.

There,
sunning himself
on a rock,
sat a big turtle!

Mr. Wolf sprang on him and cried,

"I've got you now, Uncle Turtle.

For I'm the clever hunter.

I've got my teeth

all long and sharp.

My fork I whittled out of wood.

My bib I wove of cockleburs and mud.

And I'm hungry for turtle soup!"

"No, no!" croaked Uncle Turtle.

"You forgot something."

"What now?"

howled Mr. Wolf unhappily.

"Your soup spoon,"

croaked Uncle Turtle.

"Whoever heard of eating soup

without a soup spoon?"

"Oh," said Mr. Wolf.
"I didn't think of that."
"Of course you didn't,"
agreed Uncle Turtle.

"Run and fetch it,
my boy.
I'll wait here
and hum a little song."
"All right," said Mr. Wolf.
"But don't hum *too loud*."

"Why not?"
asked Uncle Turtle.
"Because you may
frighten yourself
and fall into the water.
Then I'd never find you
because I can't swim."

"In that case
I'll hum softly,"
promised Uncle Turtle.
"Mind the soup spoon
doesn't leak,"
he called
as Mr. Wolf was leaving.

43

THUMP THUMP THUMP

Mr. Wolf sat on the
doorstep of his hut,
pounding a handle
on a nutshell.
This would be his soup spoon.

He filled it with water
to make sure it didn't leak.
No, it would
do very well.
Uncle Turtle
would be pleased.

In a twinkling
Mr. Wolf was back at the pond,
wearing his bib
and holding his fork and soup spoon.
But where was Uncle Turtle?
Circling the pond,
he called,
"Uncle Turtle, I'm back.
Where are you humming?"
No one answered.
But a strange, bubbly sound
came from under the water.
It was Uncle Turtle!
He was laughing
as he watched Mr. Wolf
from his hiding place in the reeds.

"Drat!" cried Mr. Wolf.
"I should never
have trusted him.
He must have fallen
off the rock,
after all.
Now he's humming to himself
under the water."

Mr. Wolf decided
he would have
nothing more to do with
such stupid water animals.
So he trotted
into the hills.

When he got there,

he stopped short and stared.

In the middle of a glen

stood a tall shiny horse!

Mr. Wolf sniffed importantly

and ran toward her.

"I've got you now, Mrs. Horse.

For I'm the clever hunter.

I've got my teeth

all long and sharp.

My fork I whittled out of wood.

My bib I wove

of cockleburs and mud.

I made a soup spoon that won't leak.

And I'm hungry

for a horse like you!"

"Hmm?" Mrs. Horse
looked up slowly.
"Well, I won't mind
if you eat me.
You must start
on my hind hooves, though.
They're as sweet as clover."

"Anything to please you,"
said Mr. Wolf politely.
First, he straightened his bib.
Then he tapped
tok tok tok
on Mrs. Horse's hooves
with his fork and soup spoon.

Suddenly—

THUD THACK THUMP!

Mr. Wolf was flying

through the air!

Mrs. Horse had kicked him
so hard
and so far
that he landed
right outside his own door.

"E-O E-O E-O-o-o-o!"
Mr. Wolf yelped.
He hurt from the tip of his nose
to the hairs on his tail.
And lying in the bushes
were his dear soup spoon,
his fork, and his bib.
Slowly he collected them
and limped into his hut.
"Foolish horse," he whined.
"She mùst have thought I was a *fly*."
For many long days Mr. Wolf stayed
at home and rubbed his bruises.
He ate the leftover roots and berries.
But soon they were gone,
and there was nothing to eat.

At night the animals peered
into Mr. Wolf's window, and
they began to feel sorry for him.
"How hungry he looks,"
clucked Mrs. Goose.
"Perhaps we ought to help him,"
said Mrs. Horse.
"Let's bring him supper,"
suggested Uncle Turtle
and Grandfather Goat.

And so every day
while Mr. Wolf slept tight,
they would creep into his hut
and leave a big bowl
of roots and berries.
Next to the bowl,
they would put
his fork and spoon and bib.

When evening came
and Mr. Wolf awoke,
he would leap upon the bowl
and gobble up the roots and berries.
"Thank you,
good spoon, fork, and bib,
for bringing me this tasty supper,"
Mr. Wolf would say politely.

Before long Mr. Wolf was
well enough to go out hunting.
For what?

For roots and berries!
First he'd tie on his bib.
Then he'd run through
a bramble patch
and catch berries on his fork.
And with his soup spoon
he'd dig up roots.

And very soon all agreed,
Mr. Wolf was the cleverest hunter
in the whole forest.

About the Author

Cynthia Jameson is the author of two *Break-of-Day* books, *The Clay Pot Boy* and *Winter Hut, Catofy the Clever,* and *A Day with Whisker Wickles,* all published by Coward, McCann & Geoghegan.

About the Artist

Ursula Landshoff studied art in Munich, Germany, and later at the Museum of Modern Art in New York City. Her illustrations appear in *Sesame Street Magazine,* and she did the delightful drawings for *Georgette,* a Coward, McCann & Geoghegan book. She has also written and illustrated two books, *Daisy and Doodle* and *Daisy and the Stormy Night.*

Mrs. Landshoff lives in New York City with her husband, who is a photographer. They spend much of their time traveling in the United States and Europe.